The Luminthral's Daughter

Written By Evan Orgren

Illustration by Aldaberto Ignacio.

Published By Arrive Ltd.
Print ISBN: 978-1-959935-10-0

Library of Congress Control Number: 2025908673

OURAY COLORADO USA

For Nina—
May you always hear the whisper in the woods and
follow your own wild path.

The Luminthral's Whisper

In the village of Thornwick, where cobblestone paths wove through thatched cottages, sixteen-year-old Elara felt the world was a tapestry too tightly woven to hold her dreams. The Luminthral forest loomed beyond the village, its ancient trees casting long shadows that seemed to beckon her. Their gnarled branches, draped in moss-like emerald veils, whispered secrets in the wind. Elara's hazel eyes lingered on their edges, searching for something she couldn't name. Beneath the rhythm of her days—weaving baskets from river reeds, foraging for herbs in the meadows, helping her adoptive mother, Mara, knead dough for the weekly market—a restless fire burned in her chest, sharp and strange, like a pulse that wasn't entirely her own.

Thornwick was a quaint village full of understated charm. Bright wildflowers speckled the fields, their hues popping against the lush spring green, while the air had the comforting aroma of freshly baked bread mixed with the damp, earthy scent of dew-soaked soil. The villagers were warmhearted, their faces etched with either smiles or concern, depending on how the harvest fared that season. Mara's hearty laughter grounded Elara, and her rough, calloused hands steered Elara through daily tasks with a tender care that felt like a true home. Still, Elara couldn't escape the feeling that she didn't quite belong.

Her dark curls, pushed back behind her ears, shimmered in the sunlight in a way that stood out against the lighter hair of most villagers, and her swift movements often sparked curious looks from those around her. At the market, old Tilda once squinted at her over a basket of apples, muttering, "No girl moves like that, sharp as a fox." A trader hefted an apple, grinning. "No fields bloom like Thornwick's—forest's doing, they say, though none dare ask why." Mara had laughed it off, calling Elara her gift, found swaddled in moss at the forest's edge as a baby. Still, her silence about Elara's birth parents was a shadow, a question mark etched into her heart. In quiet moments, Mara's gaze would drift to the forest, a flicker of dread crossing her face.

The village noticed Elara's differences more than Mara admitted. During a spring festival, Elara's arrow struck the archery target's center, outshining boys twice her size. The crowd clapped, but whispers followed—Widow Ren called her "forest-touched," half in jest, and young Cal frowned, saying, "She aims like she's hunting something we can't see." Mara squeezed her shoulder then, her smile tight, and changed the subject to bread prices. Elara felt their eyes, not cruel but heavy, marking her as Thornwick's oddity. Their words stung, a quiet reminder of the distance between her and the village she loved—she wanted to belong, to be more than their whispers. She didn't resent them; she loved the village's cobblestones, laughter, and fields blooming under a brighter sun than in tales of distant lands. Yet the Luminthral's call was louder, tugging at a part of her she didn't understand.

Her father's old bow was her solace. She could still recall his warm laugh, the way he'd guided her tiny hands to grip the bow's curve, whispering, "Steady, my little arrow," as they aimed at a straw target in the meadow. He'd died when she was four, leaving a worn yew bow and a quiver of arrows fletched with goose feathers. At dusk, Elara practiced in the meadows, the bow's curve familiar under her fingers. She'd nock an arrow, draw the string taut, and let it fly, the thud against a straw target grounding her. Sometimes, as the arrow soared, a faint ache bloomed in her chest—not pain, but a pressure, like a seed straining for light. It faded when she turned from the forest, leaving her unsettled. The village boys watched from afar, whispering about her aim, but none approached. Elara didn't mind. Solitude let her hear the Luminthral's murmurs—a distant song tugging at her soul, sharper when the ache stirred.

Mara's stories fueled her imagination. By the hearth's glow, Mara spun tales of the Verdant Kin—mythical guardians with skin like polished jade and eyes glowing like fireflies. "They speak to the trees," Mara's voice softened, her eyes distant. "Some say the forest chooses its own, a child born of its light, their heart pulsing with its song—a spark only the Luminthral can wake." Elara's chest tightened, the ache flaring as if the story knew her name. Elara hung on every word, picturing herself among them, her arrows tipped with starlight. Mara's tale darkened one night—she spoke of a guardian who fell to greed, seeking to bind the forest's heart for himself. "He spawned shadows," she said, her eyes distant, "a rot that hunts the green. They say he meant to save the forest once, a scholar who loved its light too fiercely, but greed twisted him into ruin. His name was Varnok."

Mara's eyes lingered on a locked drawer, her voice faltering at the mention of a guardian's name as if guarding a secret heavier than her needle. She paused, her needle still in the mending, then shifted to lighter tales of dancing vines. Elara's pulse quickened, the chest ache flickering, but Mara's worried glance silenced her questions. The stories held truths she couldn't share, ones Aeloria had whispered in desperation as she handed over the moss-swaddled babe—a warning of a shadow born from greed, a rot that could one day come for her daughter.

Thornwick's fields were its pride, their harvests richer than villages beyond the hills, or so the traders said. Elara noticed it in the market—apples heavy with juice, wheat stalks tall as her waist, wildflowers that bloomed even in late frost. Mara once remarked, kneading dough, that the land's bounty seemed tied to the Luminthral's shadow, thriving as if blessed. Elara wondered at it, gathering herbs by the forest's edge, where the soil felt warmer under her fingers. The thought lingered, a thread connecting her village to the trees that called her, though she couldn't say how. Elara's fingers brushed the warm soil. The ache in her chest flared, a pulse like a heartbeat echoing from the trees as if they knew her name.

One stormy night, everything changed. Elara woke with a start, her heart pounding as if it sought to escape her ribs. The ache in her chest was sharper now, a pulse that matched the thunder outside. A dream lingered, vivid and sharp: she stood in a glade, rain-slick leaves brushing her skin, as a voice like rustling branches called her name. Green light pulsed from a towering tree, its roots curling toward her like beckoning fingers, promising answers. She lay still, the dream's echo drowning out the storm. Rain battered the shutters, wind howling through Thornwick's lanes, but the forest's call was stronger. It wasn't just a dream—it was a summons. Her fingers brushed the bow by her bed, her father's warm laugh echoing in her memory. Thornwick had been her shield, Mara, her anchor, but the ache in her chest was a fire she couldn't douse. Staying meant smothering it; leaving meant facing the unknown.

She rose, her bare feet cold against the floorboards. The cottage was dark, and Mara snored a soft rhythm from the next room. Elara pulled on her woolen cloak, its hem frayed from years of use, and laced her boots, the leather creaking softly. Her bow and quiver rested by the door as if waiting. She hesitated, glancing at Mara's room. Leaving felt reckless—Widow Ren's words, Tilda's squint, and

Mara's quiet defenses flashed through her mind. Thornwick was her home, yet staying felt like betraying the fire in her chest, the ache that urged her forward. With a deep breath, she slipped outside, the storm swallowing her silhouette.

The Luminthral was a world unto itself. Lightning cracked the sky, illuminating trunks twisted like ancient dancers frozen mid-step. The rain stung Elara's face, soaking her cloak, but she pressed deeper, her boots sinking into the mud. Despite the season, the air smelled of wet earth, pine, and something sweeter, like blooming jasmine. The ache in her chest pulsed stronger, guiding her like a beacon. She moved by instinct, the dream's glade pulling her forward. Branches snagged her sleeves as if testing her resolve, but she pushed through, her breath visible in the chill.

Hours blurred, the storm easing to a drizzle that pattered on leaves. Elara's legs throbbed, her quiver bumping against her hip, but turning back was unthinkable. The forest felt alive, its presence a weight on her shoulders. She paused to catch her breath, leaning against a tree. Its bark was warm under her palm, pulsing faintly, and for a moment, she swore it whispered her name. The ache flared, a warmth spreading through her, not pain but promise. She shivered, not from cold but from a truth she couldn't yet grasp.

A flicker of light caught her eye, faint through the trees. She followed it, her steps cautious, until she reached a clearing bathed in moonlight. Clouds parted, moonlight spilling over a towering tree, its bark etched with runes that flickered like firelight on water. Their hum, low as a distant stream, matched the ache in her chest, now a warm thrum beneath her ribs. Roots sprawled like rivers, moss soft underfoot. Elara's breath caught the dream's glade now real before her. The air hummed, charged with energy that raised the hair on her arms.

Movement stirred the shadows. A figure stepped into the light—tall, cloaked in vines that shifted like living armor. His skin gleamed like polished jade, his eyes twin emeralds glowing with quiet intensity. A wooden staff rested in his hand, its tip carved with spirals that seemed to writhe. Around his neck hung a pendant—a simple silver chain with a small emerald shard, its faint glow a pale echo of the tree's runes. Elara's fingers tightened on her bow, her pulse racing, the ache easing as if soothed by his presence. This was no hunter, no villager. He was something else entirely.

She nocked an arrow, her voice steady despite her fear. "Who are you? Why are you here?"

The figure raised a hand, palm open, his gaze calm but piercing. "I am Torin of the Verdant Kin—we are guardians who breathe the forest's magic. And you, Elara, are not what you seem."

Her arrow wavered. "How do you know my name?"

"The Luminthral speaks," Torin said, his voice a low hum, like wind through reeds. "It has watched you since you left at its edge, its roots whispering your name each time you ventured near, your presence a light it couldn't ignore."

Elara's mind reeled. Mara's silence, the stories of fallen guardians, and her own restlessness all collided in a rush of questions. The ache in her chest pulsed faintly as if answering him. "My parents? Mara never—"

"Mara swore to keep you safe," Torin interrupted gently, his staff tapping the moss softly, grounding his words. "Your parents, Aeloria and Varen, guarded the Heartgrove, a glade where the forest's magic breathes. But the Greled—creatures of rot, born from a guardian's betrayal to devour the forest's light—hunted us. They gave you to Mara to shield you from their wrath."

Torin's gaze drifted to the pool, his staff trembling slightly. "I was there when Aeloria fell," he said, voice low. "She begged me to protect the Heartgrove, but I hesitated—too slow to stop the Greled's claws. Her light faded in my arms." His emerald eyes met Elara's, steady but haunted. "When the forest called you, I swore I'd not fail her daughter. You're her hope, Elara—and mine."

The words were a blade, cutting through years of wondering. Elara's bow lowered, her hands trembling.

Mara's worry, Tilda's mutters, the village's glances—had they all sensed what she hadn't? "Why didn't she tell me? Why now?"

"The forest chose this moment," Torin said. "A shadow grows, born of a guardian's greed, and the Heartgrove weakens. Your dream was its call, Elara. You're needed."

She opened her mouth to argue, but a guttural hiss split the air. Red eyes flared from the trees, five pairs glowing like embers. The Greled emerged—squat, twisted creatures with bark-like skin cracked and oozing, claws like blackened thorns. Their stench hit her like a wave, rotting fruit and decay choking her throat. Elara's stomach churned, the ache in her chest flaring as if in warning, but she raised her bow, instincts honed by meadow practice.

Torin's staff glowed green, vines coiling around it. "Stay behind me," he ordered, his calm replaced by steel.

"No," Elara said, her voice firm despite the fear clawing her chest. "I can fight."

Torin's eyes flicked to her, a glint of respect in them. "Then aim true."

The Greled charged with claws slashing through the mist. Torin spun his staff, sending arcs of green light that slammed one into a tree, bark splintering. Elara loosed an arrow, her hands steady despite the ache pounding faster. It struck a Greled's shoulder, black ichor spurting.

The creature snarled, lunging, but her second arrow found its chest, and it crumpled. Together, they felled three Greled, their movements a desperate dance of light and steel, the ache in her chest a rhythm guiding her aim.

"You have a spark in you!" Torin remarked as he severed the head of a Greled. "You're quicker than any human I've met."

Elara glanced briefly at Torin, about to respond. A claw grazed Torin's left arm, tearing through the vines of his cloak and into flesh, blood welling dark against his jade skin. He staggered, blood dripping, his light dimming. Elara's heart lurched—she barely knew him, yet losing him felt like losing Mara, the village, everything familiar. She fired again, driving a Greled back, but another swiped at her cloak, ripping fabric. Torin stumbled, his staff slipping from his right hand, but his voice cut through the chaos. "Run!"

He shoved her toward the trees with his uninjured arm. Elara hesitated, her eyes locked on his wound, the ache urging her to stay. But fear won, and she sprinted into the forest, the Greled's hisses fading, drowned by her pounding heart. She wove through brambles, branches snapping underfoot, her breath ragged with guilt—had she left him to die? She stopped, gasping, the clearing lost to sight, her hands trembling as she gripped her bow, the ache in her chest a quiet reprimand.

A rustle made her spin, arrow nocked, but it was Torin, limping and pale, his hand clutching his arm. Blood seeped through his fingers, dark against his jade skin. "You're hurt," Elara said, rushing to him, guilt twisting her gut.

"I'll live," he rasped, his voice strained but resolute. "We must reach the Verdant Kin's sanctuary. The Greled won't stop."

Elara nodded, slinging his arm over her shoulder. His weight was heavy, but she bore it, her jaw set. The forest seemed to shift, aiding them—fireflies lit their path, their glow soft as candlelight, branches parting like curtains. Her mind churned with Torin's words: her parents, the spark, the Greled. Fear and wonder warred within her, but one truth burned bright—she was part of this, woven into the forest's song as surely as Thornwick's fields were to its bounty.

As they stumbled deeper into the Luminthral, the storm's last whispers faded, leaving only the forest's melody. Elara felt it in her bones, a rhythm of life and secrets, pulsing with the ache that marked her as more than Thornwick's daughter. Whatever lay ahead, she'd face it—not as the village's outcast, but as a daughter of the Verdant Kin, ready to claim her place.

The Kin's Sanctuary

The Luminthral's dawn broke in hues of gold and amber, filtering through the canopy as Elara supported Torin toward a waterfall that roared like a living beast. Its mist, cool and sharp, kissed her face, washing away the night's terror but not its weight. Her cloak was heavy with rain, her boots caked in mud, and Torin's arm across her shoulders felt like a vow she hadn't meant to make. His wound, no longer bleeding, left him pale, his jade skin dulled to weathered stone. The Greled's red eyes haunted her, their stench a bruise in her memory. Yet the forest's song—soft hums of wind and distant birdcalls— urged her forward as if it trusted her even when she doubted herself.

Torin paused before the waterfall, his breath uneven. He murmured a word, sharp and melodic, and vines cloaking the rock parted like curtains drawn by invisible hands. A tunnel yawned beyond, its walls aglow with bioluminescent moss pulsing green as new leaves. Elara's breath caught, her exhaustion forgotten. The air was cool, scented with earth and honeyed blossoms. She helped Torin forward, her boots echoing on stone, each step pulling her deeper into a world she'd only dreamed of, the ache in her chest from the night before now a faint warmth, stirring with the moss's glow.

The tunnel widened into a cavern as vast as a cathedral, its ceiling studded with crystals glittering like a starfield trapped in stone. Verdant Kin moved through the space, their forms graceful and varied—some tall as saplings, others sturdy as oaks, their skin shimmering in emerald, jade, and olive shades. Their eyes glowed softly, reflecting the cavern's light, their voices weaving a symphony of murmurs and laughter. Glowing plants lined the walls, petals unfurling to release motes of light drifting like fireflies. At the cavern's heart lay a pool, its surface mirror-smooth, reflecting a tree of pure light pulsing with a rhythm Elara felt in her bones. The sight stole her breath, her hazel eyes wide with wonder.

Three Kin approached, their presence commanding despite their silence. Lira, lean and sharp-eyed, carried a bow carved with vines, her gaze pinning Elara like an arrow. Her hair, braided with leaves, swayed as she tilted her head, assessing. Kael, broad and scarred, gripped an axe gleaming like moonlit water, his expression stern but not unkind. Nyra, a healer, radiated calm, her hands glowing faintly with warmth that eased the air. Torin straightened, pain flickering across his face, and introduced Elara with a voice steady as stone.

"She is Aeloria's daughter," he said. "The forest called her to us."

Lira's eyes narrowed, fingers tightening on her bow. "A village girl?" Lira snapped, bow taut in her grip. "What's she got but straw and dreams to offer us?"

"The spark proves it," Torin replied, unyielding. "She fought the Greled at my side, held her ground when many would've fled."

Nyra knelt by Torin, her hands hovering over his wound. Green light flowed, knitting flesh with a soft hum, the air briefly scented with fresh-cut herbs. Nyra's brow furrowed, her hands trembling as she channeled the sanctuary's magic, whispering to the forest for strength to pull Torin back from the rot's edge. She exhaled shakily, a shadow crossing her face as the glow faded— her magic steady, but her eyes betrayed a flicker of doubt, as if the forest's strength came at a cost she feared she couldn't always pay. "She's brave," Nyra said, glancing at Elara with a smile like sunlight. "But courage alone doesn't make her ready."

Elara stepped forward, her chin lifting under their scrutiny. Her bow hung at her side, its curve grounding her like Mara's hands kneading dough. "I don't know what I'm ready for," she admitted, her voice clear in the cavern's hush. "But I'm here. I want to understand—my parents, the forest, all of it."

Kael's grunt was low, almost a laugh, his scarred face softening. "She's got spirit. Let's see if it holds."

Torin gestured to the pool, its light rippling across his face. "This is the Echo Pool," he said. "It holds the forest's memories—joys, sorrows, battles. Look, Elara, and see."

Elara met Torin's gaze, her heart pounding with a mix of fear and resolve. She nodded, stepping forward as the Kin parted silently. Their eyes were a mix of curiosity and reverence, giving her space to face the forest's truths.

Elara approached, boots silent on moss, and peered into the water.

Images swirled, vivid as dreams: Kin dancing under starlight, laughter chiming as vines wove crowns. They crafted spells, coaxing trees to bend, hands glowing emerald. Then darkness crept in—Greled tearing through glades, claws blackening leaves, trees withering to ash. A woman appeared, her face so like Elara's it stole her breath. This had to be Aeloria, her mother. Aeloria, cradling a baby, stood in a burning glade, eyes fierce with love and fear. At the same time, beside Aeloria, a male she could only assume was her father, Varen, was engaged in combat with Greled. Varen fought, his jade skin aglow, a spear in hand that hummed with runes, its tip carving arcs of light to hold back the Greled's claws. She whispered a spell, green light flaring, and the baby vanished in moss and starlight.

The pool rippled, this time showing Aeloria in a glade. *Her hands glowed as she fastened the pendant around her neck. "It drinks your spark to wield the Heartgrove's light,"*

Aeloria said, her voice taut in the vision. Elara's chest tightened, the ache stirring as if it recognized the warning. *"Push too far, and it locks your magic into the Lunarcore—a safeguard to save the forest, even if it means losing your power. You'd feel its song but wield nothing."*

Varen's jaw tightened. "And if the forest calls it back?" Aeloria's eyes dimmed. "Only its deepest need could wake a sealed spark. Few return."

Elara's throat tensed, fingers curling into fists. "That baby was me," she whispered, the truth a weight she craved and feared. Her chest tightened, not with the ache but with a flood of longing and loss—she'd spent years dreaming of parents who might explain her restlessness. Now they were real, their love a fierce light in a burning glade, yet gone before she could know them. A tear slipped down her cheek, for Aeloria's intense eyes, for Varen's unknown strength, for a life she'd never lived but felt in her bones.

Another image flickered—Varen, standing tall in a sunlit glade, teaching young Kin to listen to the forest's rhythm through his spear's runes. His voice, steady as a river, guided them to sense danger in the soil's tremors, a skill that had once saved the Heartgrove from a hidden blight. His patience mirrored Aeloria's fire, a balance that made them the glade's shield.

Torin's hand rested lightly on her shoulder. "Aeloria and Varen died to save you. The Greled seek the Heartgrove, a glade where a crystal tree channels the forest's magic. If they corrupt it, the Luminthral falls—and with it, lands far beyond, their rivers and fields bound to our roots. Its roots feed lands you've never seen, their bounty tied to our care."

A tear slipped down her cheek, for Aeloria's intense eyes, for Varen's unknown strength, for a life she'd never lived but felt in her bones. She stood frozen, the pool's light steady, her chest heavy with a longing she couldn't voice—a life so close, yet lost to her. Her mind spun, Mara's silence a deeper wound. A memory surfaced—Mara, years ago, hesitating by the locked drawer after a storm, whispering, "Not yet, little one," as she tucked away the green stone, her hands trembling as if it burned. Elara had thought it a game then, but now the drawer felt like a door to answers she wasn't ready to face.

Had Mara kept her safe or kept her from herself? Anger flickered—years of wondering and feeling out of place might have been eased with the truth. Yet Mara's warm laughter, her calloused hands guiding Elara's hands through dough, whispered love, not betrayal. Elara's heart twisted, torn between resentment and gratitude, knowing she'd need to face Mara to understand. The mention of distant lands echoed Mara's words about Thornwick's bounty, stirring memories of warm soil under her fingers. "Why me? What's this spark?" Elara whispered to herself.

Elara's gaze drifted to a stone pedestal, where a necklace rested—a green gem set in silver, its glow matching the moss. "The spark is a fragment of your soul, tied to the Heartgrove's power, passed by your parents," Torin replied to the whispered questions he overheard. "It can grow or wane, but its root is yours alone. Only one with it can wield the pendant safely. It amplifies our magic but demands control."

Seeing Elara's gaze, Torin nodded towards the pendant. "The Verdant Pendant, it's all we have left from Aeloria. We recovered it from Thornwick years ago. A thief, drawn by the pendant's pull, stole it from a cottage one night, but our scouts tracked it down, sensing its magic before it could fall into darker hands."

Elara's eyes lingered on the pendant, its light stirring warmth in her chest, restless as the ache from her village days. She reached out, but Nyra's gentle hand stopped her. "Not yet," Nyra said, firm but kind. "Its power could overwhelm you. We need to train you first." Elara nodded, the pendant's call lingering like a half-remembered song.

The morning mist clung to the training glade, a hidden pocket of the Luminthral where ancient trees arched overhead, their branches heavy with swaying targets carved from bark. Elara's boots sank into the moss, the air sharp with pine and the faint sweetness of blooming starflowers. Her father's bow felt heavy in her hands, a familiar weight that anchored her as Lira strode ahead, her own bow carved with curling vines, her emerald eyes glinting with a challenge. The other Kin lingered at the glade's edge, their murmurs a soft hum, watching the village girl with curiosity and doubt.

"Village aim's too stiff for this," Lira said, her tone sharp as she nocked an arrow, her movements fluid as water. She loosed it without looking, the arrow arcing through the mist to strike a target dangling from a high branch, its thud echoing through the glade. "Show me what you've got, Elara."

Elara's fingers tightened on her bow, the ache in her chest stirring—not the spark, but a flicker of unease. She'd hit straw targets in Thornwick's meadows a thousand times, but these moved with the wind, their rhythm alien. The Kin's eyes weighed on her, Lira's most of all, and she felt the distance between her human hands and their forest magic. But she wouldn't falter. She stepped forward, her breath steadying as she recalled a trick from Thornwick—listening to the wind through the reeds to judge its direction.

"Watch the wind," Elara said, her voice quieter than intended. She tilted her head, closing her eyes for a moment to hear the forest's breath—the rustle of leaves, the faint whistle through the branches. Her arrow nocked. She drew the string taut, the yew creaking softly, and loosed it. The arrow sailed, cutting through the mist, and struck the edge of the target, a hair from the center.

Lira smirked, her arms folding as her braid of leaves shifted with the movement. "Better than I expected... for someone raised in a village." Her eyes flickered with surprise, a grudging respect that warmed Elara's chest. Her human roots had offered something new, a bridge between Thornwick's simplicity and the forest's complexity.

"Again," Lira said, stepping closer, her voice softer but no less demanding. She pointed to a target half-hidden behind a curtain of vines, its surface barely visible. "This time, feel the forest's pulse. It's alive, Elara. It'll guide you if you listen."

Elara nodded, her heart pounding as she tried to sense what Lira meant. She closed her eyes again, her fingers brushing the bow's curve, and focused. The ache in her chest flared, a warmth that wasn't just memory—it was the forest, its rhythm humming through the ground, up her legs, into her bones. The vines rustled, a faint pulse like a heartbeat, and she loosed the arrow. It curved through the air, threading the vines to strike the target dead center.

Lira nodded slightly, but her lips twitched, a rare approval that felt like a victory. "Better," she said, her tone lighter. "You might survive here yet."

Elara smiled, the ache settling into a quiet glow, her place among the Kin a little less distant. But as Lira turned to set another target, Elara's smile faded—she'd hit the mark. The forest's magic felt like a language she'd never fully talk, leaving her caught between two worlds, belonging to neither.

Lira taught her to sense the forest's pulse, arrows curving through obstacles to find hidden marks. Lira's rare nods felt like victories. During a drill, a target snagged high in a thorny vine, out of reach. The Kin hesitated, unused to such obstacles. Still, Elara recalled Thornwick's harvest— using a forked stick to pluck apples from high branches. She fashioned a tool from a fallen branch, hooking the target down. Lira's brow arched a flicker of respect. "Clever, village girl," she said, and Elara smiled, her human roots proving their worth in the forest's heart.

But Lira's wariness lingered. One evening, Elara overheard her speaking to Torin by a glowing fern. "A human among us?" Lira said, voice low. "What if she dilutes what we are? Years ago, human hunters burned a glade my sister loved, laughing as the flames took her refuge—she barely escaped, and I swore I'd never trust their kind again." Torin's reply was calm: "She's half human. I grew up with her father, Varen was strong and a brave soul. Don't forget! Aeloria was the first human the Luminthral allowed into our sanctuary. She was more powerful than any of us. The forest chose Elara, Lira.

Trust its voice." Lira fell silent, her gaze distant, and Elara felt a pang—not anger, but a resolve to prove her place.

***

Lira slipped away, a bow slung across her back, to a quiet glade beyond the cavern. Charred stumps lingered, remnants of a fire that her sister, Taryn, had barely escaped—human hunters' laughter still echoed in Lira's memory, their torches a scar on the forest she'd sworn to protect. Lira knelt, fingers brushing a blackened root, her jaw tight. "Never again," she whispered, but Elara's arrow at the mock ambush flashed in her mind—a human's skill, steady as any Kin's.

***

The cavern's sparring ring glowed faintly, bioluminescent moss casting a soft green light over the stone floor, slick with condensation. Elara gripped a wooden staff, its runes warm under her palms, her breath visible in the cool air as Kael circled her, his axe gleaming like moonlit water. His jade skin bore scars that caught the light, a map of battles Elara could only imagine, and his amber eyes held a sternness that made her stomach tighten. The Kin watched from the cavern's edges, their silhouettes a quiet audience, their whispers a low hum that echoed off the crystal-studded ceiling.

"Strength isn't muscle," Kael growled, his voice rough as he lunged, axe swinging in a low arc toward her legs.

Elara jumped back, her staff meeting his axe with a sharp crack, the impact jarring her arms. She stumbled, her boots slipping on the stone, and Kael pressed forward, knocking her flat with a swift strike to her side. She hit the ground hard, air rushing from her lungs, the moss's glow blurring above her.

"Get up," Kael said, his tone unyielding but not unkind. He extended a scarred hand, pulling her to her feet with a grip like iron. "It's knowing when to stand."

Elara's side ached, her breath ragged, but she nodded, wiping sweat from her brow. Her spark flickered, a faint warmth that steadied her, but it wasn't enough—she needed more than magic to match Kael's strength. She thought of Thornwick, hauling river-reed baskets under Mara's watchful eye, the weight building her endurance. She tightened her grip on the staff, her jaw set, and faced him again.

When Kael swung, she parried this time, the staff's runes flaring briefly as she deflected the blow. Her arms burned, but she held her ground, her boots planted firm on the stone compendium, the staff's runes glowing faintly as she pushed back against Kael's axe. Kael paused, his axe lowering, a slight look of surprise in his eyes.

"Better," he said, Kael's scars catching the cavern's glow. "My brother, Ryn, loved carving runes," he said, voice rough. "He followed me on a patrol, too young. I missed the rot's signs, and Greled took him. His last rune was for courage." His voice was gruff but warm, a rare grin tugging at his lips. His eyes held Elara's. "You've got his grit, kid. Don't waste it."

Elara's chest warmed at the praise, her breath steadying as she met his gaze. The ache in her chest pulsed, not with magic but with a quiet pride—she was learning, growing, and proving herself in a world she'd only dreamed of. But as Kael stepped back, readying for another round, she wondered—could grit alone make her one of them?

***

The Echo Pool shimmered at the heart of the Verdant Kin's sanctuary, its mirror-smooth surface reflecting the radiant tree of light that pulsed above, a steady heartbeat of gold and emerald that seemed to hum through the cavern's crystal-studded ceiling. Elara knelt on the mossy edge, the air cool and scented with honeyed blossoms, a faint mist rising where the pool's light kissed the stone. The cavern's bioluminescent moss cast a soft glow, weaving shadows across Nyra's sapphire eyes, which held a calm that felt like a balm after the intensity of Lira's archery drills and Kael's sparring ring. Yet beneath Nyra's steady presence, Elara sensed a quiet weight—a flicker of doubt in the healer's gaze, as if the forest's magic she wielded came at a cost she rarely spoke of.

Nyra sat cross-legged beside her, her healer's hands resting on her knees, glowing faintly with a warmth that seemed to ripple the air. A small fern lay between them, its fronds curling inward, edges browning with a faint trace of rot—a remnant of the Greled's corruption that had crept into even the sanctuary's edges. "Healing isn't just about power," Nyra said, her voice soft as the moss beneath them but firm with purpose. "It's about listening. The forest speaks through every leaf, every root. Elara, your spark can hear it if you let it breathe."

Elara's fingers hesitated over the fern, her chest tightening with the familiar ache—not the restlessness of Thornwick, but the spark Torin had named, a warmth stirring beneath her ribs, alive and eager. She thought of Mara grinding mint for salves in Thornwick's warm kitchen, the sharp scent filling the air as Mara's hardened hands guided her own, teaching her to feel the leaves' texture for freshness. That memory steadied her now, linking her village roots to the forest's magic, but the spark felt wilder here, a flame flickering too close to a wildfire. "I don't know how to control it," Elara admitted, her voice small, her hazel eyes meeting Nyra's. "What if I make it worse?"

Nyra's smile was gentle, but her eyes held a shadow—a memory of her mother, the sanctuary's greatest healer, whose light had faded saving a wounded Kin, her hands glowing too bright as Nyra watched, helpless. "You won't," she said, her voice steady despite the flicker of grief. "The spark is part of you, Elara, but it's not all of you. Let it breathe, not burn." She placed her glowing hands over the fern, demonstrating. Her fingers traced the air above the fronds as if coaxing a melody from the forest itself. The glow spread, soft and warm, and the fern's fronds unfurled slightly, their edges greening as the rot receded, the air briefly scented with fresh-cut herbs.

"Now you," Nyra said, her hands retreating, leaving the fern half-healed, its fronds still trembling. "Close your eyes. Feel the forest's pulse, like you did with Lira's targets. It's the same rhythm."

Elara nodded, her breath steadying as she closed her eyes, her fingers hovering over the fern. The cavern's hum filled her senses—the drip of water from the ceiling, the faint rustle of glowing petals unfurling on the walls, the steady pulse of the Echo Pool's light. The ache in her chest flared, a warmth spreading down her arms into her fingertips as if the forest had reached for her. She felt the fern's life, a fragile thread trembling beneath the rot, and her spark answered, a soft glow blooming in her palms, mirroring Nyra's. The light was unsteady, flickering like a candle in a draft, and the fern's fronds twitched, greening further. A single leaf curled tighter, browning at the edges.

Elara's eyes snapped open, her breath hitching as she pulled her hands back, the glow fading. "I—I pushed too hard," she said, her voice trembling, the void of failure sharp in her chest. She saw the browned leaf, a small wound where she'd meant to heal, and her thoughts spiraled—Mara's salves had never failed, but this magic, this spark, felt too big, too wild for her hands.

Nyra's hand rested on her shoulder, her touch warm and grounding, a mirror to the love she'd once felt from her own mother before she'd faded. "You felt it, didn't you?" Nyra said, her voice gentle but firm. "The forest's life, its pain. That's the first step. Healing isn't about forcing the light but guiding it like a river finding its path." She paused, her sapphire eyes softening with a vulnerability Elara hadn't seen before. "I struggled too, once. My mother… she was the sanctuary's greatest healer. I watched her save a Kin, her bright light filling the cavern, but it took everything—her spark, her life. I was too young to help and swore I'd be as strong as her. But every time I fail, I feel her slipping away again."

Elara's throat tightened, her hand reaching to cover Nyra's, and the shared grief was a quiet bridge between them. "You're enough, Nyra," she said, echoing the words Nyra had once given her, her voice steady despite the ache. "You're here. That's what matters."

Nyra's smile was faint but grateful, her glow steadying as she squeezed Elara's hand. "And so are you," she said. "Try again. Slower this time. Let the forest guide you."

Elara nodded, her heart pounding as she closed her eyes again, her fingers returning to the fern. This time, she focused on the rhythm—the pool's pulse, the fern's fragile life, the memory of Mara's steady hands. The spark flared again, softer now, a gentle warmth that flowed like a stream, not a flood. The glow spread, the fern's fronds unfurling fully, their edges greening as the rot faded completely, the air scented with a faint hint of mint—a whisper of Thornwick in the forest's heart.

Elara opened her eyes, her breath catching at the sight of the healed fern, its fronds vibrant and alive. A quiet pride bloomed in her chest, the spark settling into a steady warmth, not a wildfire. She looked at Nyra, her hazel eyes bright with wonder. "I did it," she whispered, a smile breaking across her face.

Nyra's nod was warm, her sapphire eyes glistening with pride. "You did," she said, her voice thick with emotion. "You're learning to listen, Elara. That's what makes a healer—what makes a Kin."

Elara's smile faltered slightly, the spark's warmth a reminder of the magic she was only beginning to understand. She felt closer to the forest, to her parent's legacy. Her doubt lingered—could she master this power before the Greled returned, before the pendant's pull tested her again? As Nyra stood, offering a hand to help her up, Elara took it, her heart lighter but her resolve firm. She'd learn for the Kin, the forest, and the parents she'd never known but felt in every beat of the Luminthral's song.

Training took a tense turn one dawn. Lira led Elara to a misty glade; targets were hidden in the fog. The lesson shifted—a rustle mimicked Greled claws, and Lira signaled silence. "Track it," she whispered, testing Elara's instincts. Elara moved, bow ready, heart pounding as she followed faint scratches on bark, the forest's pulse guiding her. A glowing moth darted past from the left, its wings shimmering unnaturally. Elara pivoted, her arrow piercing its wing—an illusion that shimmered and faded, a Kin's trick, not a Greled. Lira nodded, sharp but impressed. "Pretty good, village girl." Elara's spark flared, her aim sharpened by Thornwick's quiet meadows.

Torin, healed but quieter, shared the Greled's history one night by a glowing fern. "They were born from betrayal," he said, voice heavy. "Varnok, a Kin scholar, sought to master the Heartgrove's power, twisting a root into decay. His relic—a corrupted rune—birthed the Greled, hungering for our magic." Elara listened, heart aching for a world she hadn't known but felt bound to protect. Varnok's name echoed Mara's tale of a fallen guardian. Varnok and his Greled. They were responsible for her parents' death.

The Kin were always preparing for an attack. It always came back to Varnok and the Greled. Ever since Elara arrived, the threat of the Greled was becoming more real, she had fought them with Torin, but her training was providing her with tools she hoped would help more than before. A scout's report that interrupted Torin lingered in Elara's mind—Greled numbers swelling beyond count, spawned by Varnok's corrupted rune, their hunger endless.

The sanctuary became home, its rhythms strange yet comforting. She slept on a moss bed, its softness cradling her. Meals around a stone table—berries tart as summer, roots roasted to sweetness, water tasting of starlight— wove her into the Kin's tapestry. Their laughter, stories of ancient glades, felt like Thornwick's market chatter, grounding her. Yet Lira's challenge lingered: "You're not one of us yet." Elara vowed to meet it, her spark a quiet fire.

At night, she returned to the Echo Pool, its memories a bridge to her parents. Aeloria's courage, Varen's strength, and their love burned through the Greled's shadow. The pendant waited, its glow pulling her. She traced its shape from afar, feeling its warmth in dreams. Was it her key to belonging—or a chain?

One evening, as fireflies danced in the cavern, Lira joined them by the pool, bowing across her knees. "You're not what I expected," Lira said softer. I thought a human would break."

Elara met her gaze, spark stirring. "I'm not just human," she said, words a quiet fire. "I'm their daughter. I'll prove it."

Lira's lips twitched, not quite a smile. "We'll see."

Elara's spark pulsed like a second heartbeat on her moss bed, the cavern's glow fading, tied to the pendant's promise and peril. The Greled loomed, Varnok's shadow heavier now. She closed her eyes, Aeloria's face in her mind, Thornwick's fields a distant warmth, vowing to be ready—not just for the Kin, but for the truth of who she was meant to be.

The Heartgrove's Fall

Two months had passed since Elara entered the Verdant Kin's sanctuary, and the Luminthral had woven itself into her soul. Once soft from Thornwick's chores, her hands were calloused—archery with Lira, staff combat with Kael, sensing the forest's rhythm with Nyra. The spark Torin spoke of grew, a warm current in her chest humming near the Echo Pool or the Verdant Pendant's pedestal. But with it came unease, a whisper of power she feared she couldn't control like the ache from her village days sharpened into something alive. The sanctuary's glow, once comforting, now felt like a spotlight, exposing her doubts to the Kin's watchful eyes.

Elara's skills had honed to a fine edge. She could loose an arrow blindfolded, guided by the forest's breath, and parry Kael's axe until sweat stung her eyes. Nyra taught her to feel life in a blade of grass, her spark flaring when focused. Yet the Greled's shadow loomed larger. Scouts reported blackened glades, trees oozing sap-like blood, streams choked with ash, and silent birds. The Kin's faces grew taut, laughter replaced by strategy. Elara's dreams held red eyes and her parents' faces—Aeloria's fierce love, Varen's resolve—urging her toward a destiny she barely grasped, Thornwick's wildflowers flickering in her mind like a distant home.

One dawn, mist curling through the cavern, Torin gathered the Kin around the Echo Pool. His staff's spirals glowed faintly, but his eyes carried a new weight. The pool's light deepened the lines on his jade skin. Elara had not discovered a leader among the Verdant Kin. Most of the Kin were free spirits, but Torin was respected.

"Varnok, the Greled's leader, moves toward the Heartgrove—a sacred glade where the forest's magic pulses strongest," he said, voice grave directing the latter end of his comments to Elara. "He seeks the crystal tree at its heart, the source of the Luminthral's life. If he corrupts it, the Luminthral dies—and with it, rivers and fields far beyond, like the golden plains of Erindir, where the Luminthral's roots once nurtured their harvests, now withering as the forest fades, starving lands we've sworn to shield. We must protect the Lunarcore, a golden orb within the tree that purifies their rot, keeping the forest's magic pure."

Elara's gaze drifted to the Verdant Pendant, its gem pulsing like a trapped star. Its call had grown stronger, syncing with her spark. "Can the pendant help?" she asked, her voice cutting through murmurs.

Torin's eyes searched hers. "It channels the Heartgrove's power. Your mother wielded it, Elara, but it nearly consumed her. It's a blade with no hilt—effective, dangerous. It seals your spark only if you surrender all restraint, a safeguard to bind what can't be tamed."

"I'm not afraid," she said, though her stomach twisted. The pendant's glow whispered strength and warning, stirring memories of Mara's caution over a hot stove—careful, or you'll burn.

Nyra stepped closer, her calm steadying. "Courage is only the start," she said. "Master yourself, or the pendant masters you."

Kael hefted his axe, scars catching the light. "Let her try. She's Aeloria's blood."

Lira's gaze lingered, bow slung across her back. "She'd better not falter," she said, challenge sharp but curious.

The Kin prepared, their movements heavy with purpose. Elara packed her quiver, her father's bow grounding her like Thornwick's cobblestones underfoot. She accepted a staff from Kael, its runes warming her palm. Torin handed her the pendant; its chain was cool. She fastened the gem over her heart, its pulse syncing with hers. Her breath caught—what if she failed them all? Thornwick saw her as forest-touched, the Kin as a human outsider. The pendant's weight felt like a test: could she be her parents' daughter, a true Kin, without losing the village girl who'd dreamed by the meadows? The spark flared, hot and wild, and she steadied her breath, recalling Nyra's lessons and Mara's herb lore—slow, deliberate, alive. The pendant was hers—for now.

They set out at first light, twenty Kin, steps silent on the forest floor. The Luminthral felt tense, the air thick with decay's sour tang. Leaves curled brown, birds gone, an eerie hush reigning. Elara walked beside Lira, shoulders brushing, their bond silent but firm. Torin led, staff a flare; Kael and Nyra flanked, eyes on shadows. The pendant's weight urged action before Elara was ready, its glow restless.

As they trekked, corruption overtook beauty. Glades of wildflowers were choked with thorny vines pulsing like veins. Trees leaned, bark cracked, weeping black sap. Elara's spark recoiled, nausea rising. "Varnok's work. He twists the forest to feed his hunger," Torin said, voice low.

Ahead, a Greled crouched by a tree, claws piercing its bark, black ichor seeping into the wood as faint runes flickered and died, the tree's life draining into the creature's maw—a hunger that sought the Heartgrove's core to devour the forest's magic entirely.

Nyra knelt by a dying fern, hands glowing to heal it. Green flickered, then faded. Her face tightened. "The rot's too deep. Only the Lunarcore can stop this."

They pressed on, rot's stench thick. Elara grazed the pendant, its warmth steadying her like Thornwick's fields in memory—vivid blooms, warm soil. Lira watched, unreadable. "You feel it, don't you?" Lira asked. "The forest's pain."

Elara nodded, throat tight. "It's screaming."

Lira's jaw clenched. "Let's make it stop."

By midday, they reached the Heartgrove—a glade where sunlight wove through a crystal tree, branches like spun glass. Its roots glowed faintly, and the Lunarcore pulsed at its core, a golden orb singing to Elara's spark. The glade was a sanctuary; the grass was soft, and the air was clean. Fireflies danced in daylight, mirroring the pendant's glow. Elara's chest ached with awe, the spark blazing as if home. Like rustling leaves, a soft whisper brushed her mind—"Daughter, you are mine"—the Luminthral's voice, ancient and warm, weaving through her thoughts as fireflies danced closer, their light a gentle caress. The Lunarcore's light lingered in the roots, a pulse promising to heal beyond this glade.

The beauty shattered. A roar erupted, and Varnok emerged, hulking, dwarfing a dozen Greled. His bark-like skin oozed, claws dripped ichor, and red eyes burned. Grass browned beneath him, his presence a wound. "You cannot stop the rot," he snarled, his voice grinding stone. "The forest is mine."

Torin raised his staff, light flaring. "For the Luminthral!" The battle erupted.

Kael charged, axe cleaving a Greled's arm, ichor spraying. Lira's arrows flew—eyes, throats, hearts—her precision a blur. Nyra wove shields of light, calm amid chaos. Elara fought beside Torin, arrows felling Greled, pendant burning, power clawing at her restraint.

Varnok targeted Torin, claws raking his chest. Blood sprayed, dark against his jade skin, and Torin fell, his staff clattering to the moss. Elara screamed, her heart lurching—Torin, who'd called her to this fight, who'd seen her as Aeloria's daughter, now bled because she hadn't been fast enough. Fury steadied her hands, her arrow striking Varnok's shoulder. Guilt and fury surged, her hands steadying as Varnok laughed, eyes locking on her. He snapped the arrow shaft in half, his rotting core visibly healing the wound before Elara's eyes.

"Aeloria's whelp," he taunted, voice venomous. "She stole my light." Elara's pendant flared, and a vision flickered unbidden—*Varnok was younger, his jade skin unmarred, knelt in a glade, carving a rune with trembling hands. "No more loss," he whispered, eyes bright with hope, the memory of his sister's burned glade haunting him—hunters' laughter, her cries as flames took her refuge. But the rune glowed too bright, shadows twisting, his desperation birthing rot. His eyes dimmed; the scholar lost to greed.*

Elara was swept back to the present by Varnok's words. "Aeloria sealed my spell. You'll pay for her sin." His words hit like a blade—Aeloria's past, tied to him. Elara's breath paused, Aeloria's fierce eyes flashing in her mind—had her mother's choice to seal Varnok's spell doomed them both? The pendant burned against her chest, urging her to act, but doubt gnawed—could she undo her mother's legacy, or would she fall to it?

Nyra dragged Torin to safety, light stabilizing him. The Greled pressed. Kael roared, axe a whirlwind, but a Greled resembling a lost Kin made him freeze, eyes haunted. The Kin near him felt his memory. For a moment, he saw Ryn, his younger brother, who'd followed him into a patrol years ago—Kael had been too brash, ignoring the rot's signs. Ryn paid the price, claws tearing him apart as Kael fled. A comrade he'd failed, Elara realized. His eyes held a story he wouldn't share, a debt she'd help him carry. A claw gashed his right leg, blood seeping through his armor as he stumbled to one knee, snapping him back from his memory. "Keep fighting!" he yelled to Elara, his axe still gripped in his left hand as he shoved her toward Torin's fallen form. Lira's quiver emptied, dagger drawn, breath ragged. Elara's spark swelled. Her pendant was blinding. Another vision hit Elara as she felt the warmth against her chest—*Varnok, Aeloria's mentor, betrayed in a glade, his eyes dimming as she sealed his rogue spell, a baby Elara crying. "Control it," Aeloria's voice echoed.*

Elara dodged a Greled's swipe, cloak tearing. The crystal tree trembled, Varnok's rot creeping closer. She sprinted to it, boots slipping, Varnok's laughter chasing. Elara's breath hitched, the pendant searing her chest as Varnok's rot closed in. Fear clawed at her—the same fear Aeloria must have felt, the pendant's power a wildfire threatening to consume her. But the Heartgrove's whisper—"*Daughter, you are mine*"—echoed, and she thought of Thornwick's fields, Mara's laughter, the Kin's trust. She couldn't fail them. Her hand closed around the Lunarcore, its warmth sunlight. The pendant flared, linking spark to the relic, power roaring—raw, untamed, a river breaking banks.

Light exploded, golden waves searing Greled to ash. Varnok staggered, claws slashing. Elara trembled, the pendant threatening to unravel her. She saw Aeloria and felt her will. "For the forest," Elara whispered, thrusting the Lunarcore. Another wave purified the glade, grass greening. Varnok howled, "I wanted to save us all!"—his voice cracking with lost hope—before staggering back, rot knitting his wounds, vanishing into the trees with a vow—"This isn't over!" Elara clutched the pendant, heart pounding.

Elara collapsed the Lunarcore and pendant dimming. Pain seared her arm, and her vision blurred, but the Heartgrove stood bright. Nyra rushed over, checking her pulse, and her voice was thick. "You're alive."

Torin, bandaged, knelt beside her, proud but shadowed. "You saved the Heartgrove, Elara."

Kael, bloodied, clapped her shoulder, his grin fierce despite his limp. "You pulled me through, village girl."

Lira pulled Elara up, eyes soft. "You didn't break," she said, a nod sealing respect.

Elara clutched the pendant, its heat lingering, heavy with Varnok's words—her mother's betrayal, his lost light. Her arm throbbed, Greled graze burning, but worse was the spark's quiet hunger, stirred by power. "He's still out there," she said, hoarse.

Torin nodded, distant. "He'll return stronger. But we held the line."

The Kin gathered their wounded, the glade's light a balm. Elara lingered by the crystal tree; Lunarcore returned, its glow hopeful. The pendant weighed heavy, a power she'd wielded—barely controlled. She thought of Mara, Thornwick's fields vivid in memory—wildflowers, laughter, a life distant yet anchoring. That girl was changing, forged by battle into someone new.

As they prepared to leave, Nyra gently cleaned Elara's wound. "The rot doesn't spread easily," she said, eyeing the pendant. Your spark saved us, but it's a fire that can burn you."

Elara nodded, her fingers brushing the gem. The Heartgrove's song filled her with life and sacrifice. Varnok's escape gnawed, his words—"I wanted to save us all"—echoing Aeloria's vision. Yet among the Kin, respect earned, she felt strength. The pendant was her mother's legacy, her burden, her key. Whatever lay ahead, she'd face it—as one of the Verdant Kin, her spark a light against the dark.

The Pendant's Price

The Verdant Kin's sanctuary pulsed with renewed life after the Heartgrove's salvation, but Elara felt no triumph. The crystal case housing the Lunarcore glowed on a stone altar, a beacon of hope, yet her heart was heavy with the Verdant Pendant's lingering heat. It hung around her neck, its green gem dim but restless, as if it had tasted her spark and craved more. Her arm, grazed by a Greled, ached beneath Nyra's bandages, a reminder of how close she'd come to falling. The cavern's bioluminescent moss cast gentle light on the Kin—replanting glowing ferns, carving runes into stone—but Elara's thoughts churned with Varnok's escape and the pendant's near-overwhelming power. A scout's warning echoed—Varnok had rallied, his rot-knitting wounds from the Lunarcore's fire spreading faster than before.

By the Echo Pool, its surface reflecting the tree of light, Elara trailed her fingers in the cool water, stirring visions of Aeloria wielding the pendant, face strained. Her spark flickered, quieter since the Heartgrove, but alive, an ember in her chest. The pendant had saved them, but at what cost? It had pulled at her essence, threatening to unravel her. Nyra's warning echoed: "Master yourself, or the pendant masters you." Elara wasn't sure she could.

Torin found her, his jade skin regaining luster, though Varnok's scars marked his chest. "You're troubled," he said, voice like wind through reeds. "The pendant weighs heavily?"

She touched the gem, warm. "It saved the Heartgrove, but I barely controlled it. What if I can't next time?"

Torin's eyes softened, words firm. "Aeloria faced that fear. She crafted the pendant to channel the Heartgrove, but it's flawed—binding the wearer's essence, draining it over time. It seals your spark's magic, cutting you from its power—forever, though some sparks have been known to slumber—while leaving your heart's tie to the forest only when you surrender all restraint. If you lose control, the spark—your magic, your connection to the forest's voice—could vanish, leaving you hollow, unable to hear the Luminthral's song or wield its power. You'd remain yourself, but the part that makes you Kin, that ties you to your parents' legacy, would be gone."

Elara's breath caught. "Seals it? Takes it away?"

Nyra joined, her calm steady. "Aeloria's safeguard," she said. "To prevent misuse, even by her. A last resort."

The words sank like stones. Elara had fought to claim her spark, to be her parents' daughter. Losing it felt like losing them again. Yet the pendant's pull was a tide she couldn't resist. "I need to be stronger," she said, voice steady despite fear. "Varnok's coming. I have to be ready."

Torin nodded. "Train. The Kin stand with you, but the pendant is yours to master."

Training refined her control, focusing on the pendant's emotional pull. Lira led Elara to a glade, a mock ambush replacing static targets. "Greled don't wait," Lira said, eyes sharp. Vines rustled, Kin disguised as foes lunging from the mist. Elara's bow sang, arrows threading chaos, guided by her spark. The pendant flared unpredictably, hands trembling, but she struck a hidden mark—a glowing moth mimicking a Greled's eye. Lira's nod was grudging but real, though her jaw tightened at the pendant's glow.

Kael's sparring was brutal. His axe stormed and was met with Elara's rune-carved staff. "Fight chaos," he growled, knocking her down. "Stand firm." A surprise attack—Kael mimicking a Greled's lunge—tested her instincts. Elara rolled, staff blocking, spark steadying her. Kael paused, axe lowered. "I lost someone once—don't let hesitation take you," he said, eyes distant, a wound shared to strengthen her. His grin, when she held ground, warmed her. The pendant's heat seeped into dreams—visions of Aeloria, hands glowing, eyes pleading control.

Nyra's lessons were a refuge, though strained. By the Echo Pool, she taught Elara to heal a petal and spark weaving light. "Life, not wildfire," Nyra said, hands steadying Elara's. But the pendant disrupted, blooming a fern too fast, petals browning. Nyra's frown deepened—

the Echo Pool flash her memory from earlier that morning. She'd failed to heal a Kin, her light faltering. "I'm not enough," Nyra whispered, voice breaking watching it a second time. The pool flashed briefly to her childhood allow, Elara a glimpse. As a child, Nyra watched her mother, the sanctuary's greatest healer, die saving a wounded Kin, her magic draining her life—Nyra had vowed to be as strong. The Echo Pool flash through Nyra attempting to heal Kin. Still, each failure felt like losing her mother again. Elara squeezed her hand, echoing Nyra's own words: "You're alive. That's enough." Nyra's smile was faint but grateful.

Over the next three weeks, Elara helped rebuild—hauling roots, carving runes, sap sticky on hands like Thornwick's dough under Mara's guidance. The sanctuary's central cavern hummed with activity, the air thick with the scent of roasted tubers and the faint tang of sap. Elara knelt by a stone table, her hands sticky with the resin of freshly cut roots, the same tackiness she remembered from kneading dough with Mara in Thornwick's warm kitchen. Around her, the Kin moved with purpose—some forged arrows, their tips glowing with rune light, while others wove armor from vines, their fingers deft and sure. But Elara's attention was on the baskets they used to haul roots, their knots fraying under the weight, strands unraveling like threads of a worn cloak.

She picked up a basket, her fingers tracing the loose weave, and a memory surfaced—Mara teaching her to braid river reeds, her calloused hands guiding Elara's smaller ones, the rhythm steady as a heartbeat. "Tight and even," Mara had said, her voice warm, "or it'll spill your harvest." Elara's lips curved, the memory a tether to Thornwick, and she glanced at Sylen, a young Kin with emerald skin brighter than the cavern's moss, her small hands struggling with a basket of her own.

"Here," Elara said, her voice gentle as she knelt beside Sylen, setting aside her basket. "Let me show you a trick." She gathered a handful of vines, their texture rough against her palms. She began to weave, her fingers moving with the muscle memory of years in Thornwick. "Cross like this, then pull tight—see? It'll hold better."

Sylen watched, her amber eyes wide, mirroring the glow of the crystals overhead. She mimicked Elara's movements, her small fingers clumsy but determined, the vines slowly forming a tighter weave. When she finished, she lifted the basket, testing its strength with a handful of roots. It held firm, not a strand slipping, and Sylen's face lit up, her smile as bright as the starflowers in the training glade.

"It works!" Sylen said, her voice chiming like a bell, and she hugged the basket to her chest, roots and all. "You're good at this, Elara."

Elara's heart warmed, the ache in her chest a quiet glow— not her spark, but something softer, a bridge between her worlds. She thought of Thornwick's meadows, the baskets she'd woven for the market. Now, in the Luminthral's heart, she was weaving again, her past strengthening the Kin's future. But as Sylen beamed, Elara's smile faltered—the pendant, tucked in her pouch, weighed heavy, its cold gem a reminder of the spark she'd lost, the magic she couldn't share with Sylen.

Nyra approached, her healer's hands glowing faintly, her calm a steady presence. She watched Sylen test the basket, then met Elara's gaze, her sapphire eyes warm. "You bring the village here," she said, her smile like sunlight shining through the canopy. "It suits you."

Elara nodded, her worlds aligning in the act of weaving. The pendant's weight lingered, a question she couldn't answer—could she be enough for the Kin without the magic that had defined her parents? Lira passed honeyed fruit one evening. "Not bad," she said, lighter. "For a village girl."

Elara smiled. "Not bad for a prickly spirit."

Lira laughed, their bond forged in sweat. Scouts brought grim news—groves ashed, rivers black, decay thick. Varnok rallied, his army swelling. Torin's council planned a final strike. Elara listened, pendant warm, knowing her burden. A scout added, "Fields beyond wither—rivers dry where the forest fades. Thornwick's wildflower meadows, once so bright, are graying, the soil cold as stone, its harvests failing for the first time in memory." Elara's breath caught, the words sinking in like a stone—

she'd always known the forest's magic touched her village, but now its decay did, too. She pictured the meadow where she'd practiced her bow, its blooms fading—her town, her home, withering with the forest she'd sworn to protect. The Luminthral's reach stretched far, like Thornwick's thriving harvests, tying her fight to a world unseen.

Nights by the Echo Pool showed Aeloria sealing Greled, face pale, Varen blazing. One vision lingered—*Aeloria whispering, "The forest is everything," spark dimming.* Elara woke gasping, pendant searing. Was this her fate? She confided in Nyra at dawn. "I want to save the forest," she said, voice small. "But I'm scared I'll lose myself."

Nyra's eyes held hers. "Fear means you're alive. Your parents chose you first. You're enough."

When Torin called the march, Elara stood ready, bow and staff at hand, pendant thrumming. Scouts had found Varnok and the Greled.

***

The Kin moved through a battlefield like forest—trees were posed like broken spines; moss had become dust. For Verdant Kin the tainted ground stung, their sparks recoiling at every step. They reached a corrupted glade, black sap bubbling. Glancing back, Elara could see the Heartgrove's light, fed by the Lunarcore's distant pulse. It shielded the glade behind them and urged Elara forward.

Varnok waited, his army vast—dozens of Greled, red eyes malice. His hulking form loomed, claws gleaming. "You bring a child?" he taunted, eyeing Elara. For a moment, his gaze softened, voice low—"I sought light she stole," he murmured, voice breaking before hardening. "Your pendant won't save you."

Elara clutched the gem. "We'll see," her voice like a blade.

The battle erupted, chaos swallowing the glade. Kael's axe carved Greled, claws gashing his shoulder. Lira's arrows flew, dagger flashing when empty, breath fierce. Nyra's shields healed mid-fight, her cry sharp as a claw raked her side. Torin's staff blazed, scars slowing him, Varnok aiming for his throat. Elara fought center, bow singing, staff meeting claws with rune-lit force. The pendant burned, urging release.

The Greled overwhelmed them. Nyra fell near the glade's edge, clutching her left side where a Greled's claw had raked deep, her shield of light flickering as she gasped. Kael knelt, axe slipping. Lira's dagger snapped, grabbing a staff, eyes wild. Torin staggered, Varnok's claws near. Elara's spark roared, pendant blinding. Aeloria's voice— *"Protect the forest."* There was no time for doubt.

A vision flashed behind Elara's eyes as the pendant burned—*Varnok, younger, his jade skin unmarred, stood in a glade, hands trembling as he carved a rune, whispering, "The Kin will thrive, no more loss." His eyes shone with hope, but a shadow flickered in them—fear of failure, of*

watching the forest burn as his sister's glade had, hunters'
laughter echoing in his memory. He pressed harder, the
rune glowing too bright; his desperation twisted the rune,
rot blooming, his noble intent consumed by greed for
power.

Elara tore the pendant free, her heart racing as she
poured everything into it—every memory of Aeloria's
fierce love, Varen's quiet strength, the Kin's trust,
Thornwick's blooming meadows. She knew the cost: her
spark, the magic that tied her to her parents, would be
gone. But the forest's song, the Heartgrove's light, the
lives beyond—they were worth it. Radiance erupted,
spark flooding like a river. Greled crumbled to ash, their
hisses silenced. Varnok lunged claws at her heart. "You'll
doom us as she did," he whispered, eyes fading, claws
faltering. For a fleeting moment, his red eyes cleared, the
malice giving way to a flicker of the scholar he'd been—
Varnok, who'd once carved runes with trembling hands,
dreaming of a forest free from harm. "I only wanted... to
save it," he rasped, voice breaking. "I saw her glade burn,
my sister... I couldn't let it happen again." The rot
consumed him, his form fraying to dust. Elara's throat
tightened a flicker of grief for the scholar he'd been, a Kin
who'd loved the forest as fiercely as her mother had, now
lost to his own ambition. She saw her mother in him, the
same love for the Luminthral, twisted by a different path.
But where Aeloria had chosen sacrifice, Varnok had
chosen power, and that choice had birthed the Greled's

hunger. "I know," she whispered, her voice steady, "but you lost the forest long ago." His form frayed, collapsing to dust, the air heavy with the rot's retreat.

Somewhere in the glade, the corrupted rune he'd carved pulsed once, then dimmed—its power fading with him, though Elara wondered if such darkness could ever truly die. Elara's spark vanished, a void where warmth was. The pendant flared one last time, its safeguard triggered—Aeloria's design to seal the spark, locking her magic into the Lunarcore to save the forest, a sacrifice that might never return. Elara fell, moss soft, world fading. The pendant slipped from her hand, its cold weight a mirror to the abyss within her. She'd saved the forest and kept Aeloria's promise, but the spark—her tie to her parents—was gone. A hollow ache whispered their names as darkness took her. A hush deeper than the forest itself, the Luminthral's song a faint echo in the void. Then—light.

Elara woke in the sanctuary, glow soft. Nyra knelt, tears streaking, hands checking her pulse. "You're alive," she whispered, hugging tight, her own wound bandaged.

Torin sat near, bandaged, relieved. "You destroyed Varnok. The forest—and lands beyond—breathe again."

Elara's hand closed on the pendant, dull, cold. "My spark," she said, breaking. "It's gone." In that hollow silence, she felt Aeloria and Varen slipping away again—not in death, but in the magic that had bound her to them. The spark had been their voice, courage, and love woven into her soul, and now it was a thread she could no longer hold. Yet as she clutched the pendant, its cold weight a mirror to her loss, she understood—this was their final gift, a sacrifice they'd made for the forest, now hers to carry.

Nyra nodded gently. "The pendant sealed its power. Aeloria's flaw triggered to stop the Greled, but your heart's tie to the forest remains."

Grief hit, deeper than words. She'd fought to be her parents' daughter, now gone. Yet the sanctuary's light, Kin's smiles, showed it wasn't for nothing. The forest sang, even without her spark. She thought of Thornwick's fields, blooming under Mara's care—proof her sacrifice reached far.

Lira approached, arm bandaged, eyes soft. "You didn't just save us. You became us."

Elara smiled. Their words were a balm. The pendant lay in her palm, the sacrifice's relic, its glow Aeloria's choice. Aeloria's face lingered via the Echo Pool. "Worth it," Elara said, steady. "For the forest."

The Kin gathered. It was the family she had earned. The sanctuary hummed, healing. Elara stood, pendant no chain. She was no magic's guardian but of memory, life. The Luminthral waited, and she'd walk it—not as a spark, but Elara, daughter of Aeloria and Varen, bound to the Kin.

The Luminthral's Guardian

Days after the battle, as the sanctuary's glow began to heal war wounds, Elara woke to a new reality—one where her spark was gone, but her purpose as a guardian was only beginning. Her body ached, bruises mapping the battle that claimed her spark. The Verdant Pendant lay cold in her palm, its green gem dull as river rock, no longer alive with the power that had thrummed in her chest. The emptiness that had contained her spark was tender, like a bruise fading under careful hands. Nyra knelt beside her, healer's touch steady, eyes glistening. "You're still here, we lost so many," she whispered, brushing a curl from Elara's forehead, voice thick with gratitude. "I couldn't lose you too," Nyra whispered barely audible, a confession that bound them closer.

Torin sat nearby, scars testifying to their fight, his jade skin regaining luster. "You ended Varnok," he said, pride and sorrow heavy. "The Luminthral lives because of you."

Elara's fingers curled around the pendant, the weight a memory of fire and sacrifice. "My spark," she said, voice breaking.

Nyra's hand covered hers, grounding. "The pendant sealed its power to stop the Greled. Aeloria's safeguard saved the forest—and you. Your heart's tie to the forest remains," Nyra said, her voice gentle but firm. "The pendant sealed its power, cutting you off from the spark's magic—perhaps forever, the Luminthral seems to love you though. You can still feel the spark's presence and song, but you'll wield no magic unless the Luminthral calls it back again."

The realization struck Elara like a gentle wave, carrying a quiet truth. Elara's chest tightened the void where her spark had been aching like a wound that wouldn't fully heal. She'd fought so hard to claim that magic, to feel her parents' presence in its warmth, and now it was gone—perhaps forever. A flicker of fear stirred: without it, could she truly be the guardian the Kin needed? But as she looked at the Echo Pool, its light, steady, and warm light, she felt Aeloria's fierce love and Varen's quiet strength in her resolve. The spark had been a gift, but it wasn't her—her heart, choices, and courage bound her to the forest, her parents, and the Kin.

Elara's gaze lingered on the Echo Pool, its still waters reflecting the radiant tree of light at the cavern's heart, pulsing with a steady, living beat. Aeloria's face seemed to float in the shimmer, her fierce love a constant beacon in Elara's mind. The spark had once been a bridge to her parents, a magical thread weaving her into their story, but even without it, she hadn't lost her connection. She was still their daughter, a true part of the Kin, her belonging rooted in blood and the journey she'd carved for herself.

Lira came closer, her arm wrapped in rough bandages, her expression softened with genuine respect. "You did more than save us," she said, her voice solid with certainty. "You're one of us now, whether you've got the spark or not."

Kael staggered over, propping his axe against the rugged stone wall. A wide, hearty grin broke across his scarred face. "The village girl's roots dig deeper than the Heartgrove itself," he said, his tone warm with pride.

Their words cloaked her, family forged in trust. Despite their scars, the Kin carried on—Lira's arm still stiff from the battle, Kael's limp a quiet reminder of his sacrifice, Nyra's hands slower but no less gentle as she tended to the wounded. Their resilience mirrored Elara's own, a shared strength binding them closer.

Elara's lips curved, her heart lighter despite grief. The sanctuary hummed—Kin tending ferns, carving runes, murmurs blending with water's drip. The Lunarcore's crystal case glowed, the forest's strength promised. Yet Elara felt her journey unfinished. The Luminthral was safe, but her place—and Thornwick's pull—called for reconciliation, a path she'd carve.

Weeks passed, Elara pouring into renewal. She hauled waterfall water, mist cooling her skin, and braided vines, fibers rough under calloused fingers once softened by Thornwick's dough. She ground herbs with Nyra, salves smelling of mint, and planted star-shaped blossoms. The

Kin's culture unfolded, richer than imagined, rituals making the sanctuary home.

The Kin circled the Echo Pool for the Song of Dawn each dawn, a chant rising like mist, low and resonant. Voices wove gratitude and strength. Torin taught Elara the lyrics, staff tapping rhythm as she stumbled through the ancient tongue. "It binds us to the Luminthral," he said, eyes bright. "Our promise to listen." Elara joined, voice hesitant, then stronger, blending with Lira's alto and Kael's steady bass; his scars softened as he sang, a warmth new since the battle. The song anchored her sparkless heart, its melody a fragile tether that reminded her of Thornwick's market chatter, grounding her in the Kin's rhythm. Yet as the chant faded, a quiet ache resurfaced, a silent reminder of all she had lost.

At dusk, the Binding of Roots wove bracelets from living vines, each knot a vow. Lira led, her voice clear, admitting to the Kin, "I doubted her, a human among us." She tied a bracelet for Elara, vines curling unity's rune, saying, "You proved me wrong." Nyra guided Elara's hands, her calm deeper since her healing struggles, tying her own bracelet with practiced grace. "It grows with you," Nyra said, leaves soft on Elara's wrist. Stories followed— guardians, singing trees—under glowing crystals, light dancing on walls.

The Rune Offering, held weekly by the Heartgrove, honored the forest—and Varnok's fall. Kin carved runes into stones, wishes for peace, growth, and resilience. Elara's rune for renewal wavered, lines uneven, carved with Varnok's betrayal in mind—a scholar's greed spawning rot. Carving her rune, Elara paused—could she be enough without the spark that defined her parents? Kael carved a rune for forgiveness, eyes distant, a weight lifted as he glanced at Elara, his trust her redemption. Torin placed hers among others, a mosaic circling the crystal tree. "It honors our mistakes," he said, voice warm. "For hope." Elara felt Varnok's shadow lift, the act tethering her to the Kin's healing history.

Training continued, sparkless but sharp. Lira taught tracking by scent, arrows finding marks through instinct. In a misty glade, Lira challenged her to hit a hidden target. "Trust your hands," she said, kind but firm. Elara's arrow struck true, Lira's nod a victory, their bond steady. Kael's sparring taught, not tested. "Heart over magic," he said, helping her up, hand steady. Elara blocked his blow, staff humming with her runes, Kael's grin earned. Nyra shared lore by the Echo Pool. "Kin are memory," she said, voice moss-soft, her calm a beacon. Elara listened, pendant in her pouch, legacy a choice.

Her role emerged—leading recruits, young Kin with eager eyes. Torin urged her, "You've walked both worlds." Elara hesitated, spark's loss a shadow, but saw trust and resolved.

The Heartgrove's glade shimmered with morning light, the crystal tree's branches casting prisms of emerald and gold across the mossy floor. Elara stood at the center, her father's yew bow a steady weight in her hands, its curve worn smooth by years of practice. Around her, a dozen young Kin formed a loose semicircle, their eyes—amber, sapphire, emerald—glowing with eager anticipation, their small bows carved with runes that pulsed faintly. The air carried the crisp scent of pine, a cool breeze brushing Elara's skin, and the faint hum of fireflies weaving through the canopy felt like a whisper of encouragement.

"Archery first," Elara said, her voice clear, though her chest tightened—not with the spark she'd lost, but with the weight of their trust. She was their leader now, sparkless but resolute, her role carved by the battles she'd survived. She nocked an arrow, the fletching soft against her fingers, and drew the string taut, her movements deliberate. "Watch the target, but listen to the forest. It'll guide you."

She loosed the arrow, its arc swift and true, striking the center of a bark target dangling from a low branch. The thud echoed, a sound as familiar as Thornwick's meadows, and the recruits murmured in awe, their voices a soft chorus. Elara stepped back, gesturing for Sylen to take her place. The young Kin's emerald skin was brighter than the glade's moss, and her small hands trembled as she gripped her bow.

Sylen nocked an arrow, her movements jerky, her amber eyes darting to the target with uncertainty. She loosed too soon, the arrow sailing wide, embedding in the moss with a soft thunk. Her shoulders slumped, her glow dimming, and Elara saw herself at that moment—the girl who'd fumbled in Thornwick's meadows, Mara's patient voice in her ear.

Elara knelt beside her, her voice gentle. "Listen, don't force. The forest is alive—it'll show you where to aim." She placed a hand on Sylen's shoulder, and the warmth of her skin reminded Elara of the Kin's magic, a magic Elara could no longer touch. A quiet grief briefly seized her, but she pushed it aside, focusing on Sylen's eager gaze.

Sylen nodded, her jaw set with determination, and tried again. This time, she closed her eyes for a moment, her breath steadying, and Elara felt the forest's pulse through the moss—a rhythm she could sense, even without her spark. Sylen loosed, and the arrow struck the target's edge, a hair from the center. Her smile bloomed, mirroring Elara's own from years ago, a joy so pure it eased the ache in Elara's chest.

"Well done," Elara said, her voice warm, her heart lighter despite the lack of spark. She was leading, teaching, and loving without magic, her parents' legacy alive in her actions. But as the recruits cheered, the pendant in her pouch felt heavier—a reminder of what she'd lost and the question that lingered: Was this enough?

Staff training filled the cavern with laughter and clacks of wood. Elara sparred lightly, teaching rhythm. To a faltering recruit, she shared her Varnok fears and grief. "Courage is choosing to fight," she said, eyes steady. During a tracking lesson, a young Kin struggled to spot a hidden trail marker in the underbrush. Elara recalled Thornwick's harvest games—searching for the smallest wildflower in tall grass to win a honeyed apple. She knelt beside the recruit, her voice gentle. "Look for what doesn't belong," she said, pointing to a bent leaf, a trick she'd learned in the village meadows. The recruit's eyes brightened, the marker found, and Elara felt her past and present weave tighter, her village roots strengthening the Kin's future. Recruits brightened Aeloria's strength in her words. Scouting with Lira guarded borders, checking rot or hunters. A snare glinted; Elara dismantled it, marking a warning rune. "We protect ours," she told Lira fiercely. Lira's nod sealed their shield.

The forest healed—glades bloomed, streams sparkled, birds sang. The Lunarcore's glow nurtured new glades, its light a heartbeat echoing through the Luminthral's roots. A scout reported rivers thriving beyond, fields green, crediting the Heartgrove. Elara smiled, her sacrifice rippling far like Thornwick's harvests. Yet Thornwick pulled, needing Mara, weaving the past into the present.

Torin sensed it, carving runes. "Thornwick shaped you," he said. "Go. The forest holds."

Elara sat by the Echo Pool, the pendant in her pouch a quiet weight. A memory stirred—Mara's laughter as they kneaded dough, the scent of baking bread filling the cottage, a warmth that anchored her through years of wondering. She needed that now to weave her past into the guardian she'd become. Rising, she slung her quiver over her shoulder, her father's bow a steady weight, and glanced at the Echo Pool's shimmering light, ready to face the answers waiting in Thornwick.

Alone, Elara trekked, bow across back, pendant pouched. The Luminthral sang—emerald leaves, jasmine air its melody, a thread Elara carried in her heart as she stepped beyond its borders. The forest's edge gave way to familiar fields. Thornwick dawned, cobblestones unchanged, wildflowers swaying in the breeze, their scent a quiet welcome. Bread's scent tugged her to Mara's door. She knocked, breath shallow. Mara answered, face crumpling with joy.

"Elara," Mara gasped, hugging her, flour and warmth. "I feared the forest took you."

Elara held tight, tears pricking. "I'm here. Sorry, I left."

The hearth's glow bathed Mara's cottage in a warm amber light, the scent of baking bread filling the air, a comfort as familiar as the cobblestones outside. Elara sat across from Mara at the worn wooden table, her hands wrapped around a steaming mug of tea, the ceramic warm against her palms. The wildflower she'd brought from the Luminthral lay by the hearth, its petals bright against the stone, a quiet bridge between her worlds. Mara's face, etched with lines of worry and love, traced Elara's every word as she recounted her journey—the Luminthral's song, the Kin's trust, her parents' sacrifice, the Greled's rot, the spark's price. Her voice was steady but searching, each word a thread weaving her past into her present.

"I thought the spark was me, Mara," Elara said, her hazel eyes meeting Mara's, and the ache in her chest was empty. "Now I'm finding who's left—who I am without it."

Mara clutched her mug tighter, her knuckles whitening, her gaze flickering with guilt and grief. The steam rose in faint wisps, curling like the mist of the Luminthral's glades, and her hands trembled, the tea sloshing gently against the rim. She opened her mouth to speak, then hesitated, her eyes darting to the locked drawer by the hearth—the same drawer Elara had seen her guard years ago, its secrets a shadow between them.

Elara's chest tightened, years of unspoken questions surging like a storm. She stood, her hands trembling as she set her mug down with a soft clink, her voice cracking. "Why didn't you tell me, Mara? I spent years feeling like I didn't belong—wondering why I was different, why the forest called me! I deserved to know who I was!"

Mara flinched, her gaze dropping to the table, a sob catching in her throat as she set her mug down, the steam rising in faint wisps. "I feared it'd call you away—to the same fate as them," she whispered, her voice breaking as memories flooded back—nights spent watching the forest's edge, dreading the day its whispers would claim her daughter. "Aeloria begged me that night, her hands trembling as she handed you over, swaddled in moss. 'Keep her safe, Mara,' she said. Her eyes were wild with fear. I'd never seen that look on her. 'The Greled can't find her.' I locked the pendant away, hoping to shield you, but a thief stole it one night—I thought I'd failed you both until the Kin brought it back. I kept this from you, hoping to keep you safe."

Elara's breath caught, her hand reaching into her pouch to touch the pendant, its cold gem a weight against her fingers. Anger flickered—years of wondering and feeling out of place might have been eased with the truth. She stepped closer, her boots soft on the floorboards, and saw Mara's trembling hands, flour-dusted apron, and the love in her tear-streaked face. The anger softened, her heart easing as she knelt beside Mara, taking her hands in hers, the calluses a mirror to her own.

"You kept me safe," Elara said, her voice steady now, the weight of her journey grounding her. "I found myself—

Mara, I'm their daughter, spark or not. And I'm yours, too."

Mara's smile was bittersweet, her hands squeezing Elara's as tears fell, the hearth's warmth wrapping them like an embrace. "Theirs—and mine," she whispered, her voice thick with love. As they kneaded dough, Elara's fingers sank into the familiar warmth, Mara's laughter a balm. The wildflower lay by the hearth, its petals bright against the stone. Elara hugged Mara, promising visits, her heart full of two homes—Thornwick's fields and the Luminthral's song. Villagers nodded, and children whispered of her bow—not oddity, but guardian. The Luminthral called, and she hugged Mara, promising visits and stepping into the forest, heart full of homes.

The Kin welcomed her, the sanctuary vibrant with life. They held a Binding of Roots, Lira leading, weaving a second bracelet, vines etched with unity. A feast followed—roasted roots, honeyed fruit, starlight water. The Song of Dawn rose, Kael's bass steady, Nyra's alto clear, Elara's voice precise, lyrics hers. Lira shared a tale of a sparkless guardian, eyes on Elara warming her.

Elara placed the Verdant Pendant on a shallow ledge within the Echo Pool, its green gem catching the water's glow, a relic of sacrifice now entrusted to the forest's memory. She knelt, whispering a vow in the ancient tongue Torin had taught her, her fingers tracing a vine from her bracelet into the water—a Binding of Roots to seal its legacy. The pool's light flared briefly, accepting the offering, as visions showed Aeloria and Varen smiling, love enduring. Its legacy was hers—her parents' choice, her choice, the forest's hope. Another vision shimmered—Varen, spear in hand, teaching young Kin to track by the forest's rhythm, his laughter deep as a river, a steady warmth that calmed their fears. His strength was patience, a trait Elara now carried, guiding her recruits with the same steady hand.

Lira found her by the pool, bow at rest. "Staying?" she teased, fond.

Elara nodded, smiling. "Home. Spark or not, I'm Kin."

Lira sat, shoulders brushing. "Good. I need you to keep me sharp."

Their laughter mingled with the hum. Torin joined, staff aglow, pride bright. "You've become the guardian Aeloria dreamed of—and more," he said, his voice warm with certainty.

Months later, Elara stood at the Heartgrove, crystal tree shimmering. Its roots pulsed, Lunarcore's glow a heartbeat. Bow ready, aim true, staff carved with courage, peace—she led recruits, scouted borders, sang Kin songs. Shadows might rise—storms, hunters, secrets. She'd face them, heart a light. Mara, Thornwick's fields, the dreaming girl lived in her, joined by Aeloria's courage, Varen's strength, and Kin's trust. The pendant's memory glowed, but Elara needed no spark. The forest whispered her name, and she answered—her heart alive to its song, sparkless but bound forever. The air carried the crisp scent of pine, a cool breeze brushing her skin, holding the faint hum of fireflies weaving through the canopy. The crystal tree's roots thrummed beneath her boots, their pulse a heartbeat she felt in her bones, a rhythm echoing ancient chants.

As she stood by the crystal tree, a faint rune flickered on its bark, symbolizing ancient chants and starlit rivers she'd glimpsed in her first forest dream. The Luminthral held secrets yet unspoken—a whisper of ancient chants that spoke of guardians before Aeloria, of a starlit river that flowed beyond the forest's edge, its waters said to hold the voices of the first Kin. Elara's heart stirred, a quiet resolve blooming as she stood by the crystal tree. As its guardian, she'd seek those truths in time, her journey far from over, the forest's song a promise of wonders yet to come.

Chronicles of the Luminthral: Origins and Shadows

The Luminthral's Genesis

Long before the Verdant Kin walked its glades, the Luminthral was born from the dreams of the First Star, a celestial entity that wept light into the earth. The First Star, a solitary being adrift in the void, yearned to touch the world below to weave a legacy that would endure beyond its fading glow. Where its tears fell, emerald roots sprouted, weaving a forest that pulsed with magic, its borders marked by ancient trees whose bark shimmered like molten jade under the moonlight. Ancient chants, sung by winds that carried the First Star's voice, shaped the Luminthral's borders, creating a realm where time flowed like a river—sometimes swift, sometimes still, its passage marked by the blooming of star-shaped blossoms that glowed only under a crescent moon. The forest's song, heard only by those it chose, echoed the First Star's longing for connection, a melody that bound the Luminthral to the lands beyond. Its magic stretched far, feeding rivers and fields with life, as seen in the golden plains of Erindir, where wheat grew tall despite drought, and the blooming meadows of Thornwick, where wildflowers defied late frosts, their harvests thriving under the forest's unseen care—a silent pact between the Luminthral and the world it cradled.

The Heartgrove's Creation:

At the Luminthral's heart, the First Star planted a seed of pure light, which grew into the crystal tree of the Heartgrove—a sacred glade where the forest's magic concentrated. The tree's branches, delicate as spun glass, refracted sunlight into prisms of emerald and gold, casting a glow that warmed the air with the scent of jasmine and pine. Its roots stretched beyond the Luminthral, touching distant lands, their glow a lifeline for the world's bounty, ensuring fields bloomed, and rivers ran clear even in the harshest winters. The Lunarcore, a golden orb within the tree, was forged by the First Star's final breath, a relic to purify any darkness that threatened the forest's light—its surface etched with runes that pulsed like a heartbeat, whispering the First Star's last wish to protect its creation. Legends speak of a starlit river hidden beyond the Heartgrove, a sacred stream born from the same light as the Lunarcore, its waters holding the voices of the first guardians. Those who knelt by its banks, it is said, heard whispers of a time when the Luminthral knew no rot, their truths a promise of the First Star's enduring legacy, a call to those who would one day seek its secrets to restore the forest's ancient harmony.

The Verdant Kin's Rise:

The Verdant Kin were born from the Luminthral's will, their jade skin a gift of the forest's magic, their eyes glowing with its light—emerald, amber, or sapphire, each hue a mark of the glade they were born to protect. They were tasked with guarding the Heartgrove, learning to speak with the trees through runes and chants taught by the forest's song, a melody that hummed in their bones. The Kin's first leader, Elithar, carved the Echo Pool to preserve the forest's memories, its waters reflecting joys, sorrows, and battles to guide future generations—its surface so still that a single drop could ripple visions of the past across its depths. Over centuries, the Kin developed rituals like the Song of Dawn, a chant of gratitude sung at first light to honor the forest's awakening, and the Binding of Roots, a vow of unity where living vines were woven into bracelets, their leaves curling with runes of loyalty. Their magic, drawn from the Heartgrove, allowed them to shape vines into shelters and heal wounds with a touch. Still, it came with a price—those who overreached risked their spark fading, a lesson etched in the early tragedy of Lirien, a Kin whose ambition to heal an entire glade drained her spark. Lirien's light faded as she knelt by a dying fern, her hands glowing too bright, leaving her hollow—a cautionary tale sung in the Kin's chants, a reminder of the balance their magic demanded. In their early years, the Kin faced threats from storms that tore through glades, forcing them to learn the forest's rhythm to predict its moods, a skill passed down through generations, as seen in Varen's teachings to sense danger through the soil's tremors.

The Greled's Corruption:

The Greled was not born of the Luminthral's light but its betrayal. Varnok, a Kin scholar, sought to harness the Heartgrove's power to protect the forest from human hunters who felled its trees for timber, their fires scarring glades he'd loved—memories of his sister's laughter in a now-ashed grove fueling his resolve. His rune, carved with noble intent on a stone beneath the Heartgrove's roots, twisted under the weight of his ambition, drawing on a forbidden chant that tapped into the Luminthral's shadows—a melody the First Star had sealed away, fearing its hunger, a darkness born from the forest's own grief for the lands it could not save. The rune birthed the Greled—creatures of rot, their bark-like skin oozing decay, their hunger an echo of Varnok's greed, their red eyes burning with malice that sought the Heartgrove's light to devour it entirely. The corrupted rune granted Varnok a twisted gift: the ability to mend his decaying form by drawing on the forest's stolen magic, a rot-knitting power that let him survive even the Lunarcore's purifying fire, though each healing deepened his corruption, his once-jade skin cracking further with every wound sealed. The Greled's creation fractured the Kin, leading to a schism where some followed Varnok, believing his vision of a forest unmarred by loss, their loyalty born from shared grief over human encroachment. In contrast, others fought to seal his corruption, a conflict that scarred the Luminthral for generations. The Heartgrove's roots trembled with the weight of the betrayal, rivers beyond its borders running black for a season, a wound felt even in Thornwick, where the harvest withered for the first time in memory, a silent cry from the forest for the Kin to heal what Varnok had broken.

About the Author

Evan Orgren is a storyteller at heart, blending rich imagination with a love for fantasy and adventure. Originally from the United States, he now lives in Zagreb, Croatia, with his family. When he's not writing, Evan enjoys exploring local forests, drawing inspiration from nature's quiet magic. *The Luminthral's Daughter* is his debut fantasy novella, born from a lifelong passion for crafting worlds where courage, loyalty, and hope shine brightest.

www.ingramcontent.com/pod-product-compliance
Lightning Source LLC
Chambersburg PA
CBHW041755180626

46815CB00019B/340